D0597395

DISCARDED

Fort Nelson Public Library
Box 330
Fort Nelson, BC
V0C-1R0

FEB - - 2008

for my jake

with special thanks to Tomi, Michael, Angela, Julie, and little Dave

also Dave S. and Marc+Bé, and Gregory+Beatrice

Copyright © 2007 by Dave Cooper.
All rights reserved.

The illustrations in this book were rendered
in pen and ink, colored digitally.
Manufactured in China.

Library of Congress Cataloging-in-Publication Data
Mumbly, Hector, 1967–
Bagel's lucky hat / a book by Hector Mumbly.
    p. cm.
    Summary: When Bagel the dog loses his lucky hat,
his friend Becky listens to him recount an outlandish
tale of how he spent his day, including interplanetary
space travel and a traveling robot.
    ISBN-13: 978-0-8118-4875-6
    ISBN-10: 0-8118-4875-2
    [1. Dogs—Fiction. 2. Cats—Fiction.
3. Outer space—Fiction.] I. Cooper,
Dave, 1967– II. Title.
    PZ7.M92312Bag 2007
    [E]—dc22
    2006032351

Distributed in Canada by Raincoast Books
9050 Shaughnessy Street
Vancouver, British Columbia V6P 6E5

10 9 8 7 6 5 4 3 2 1

Chronicle Books LLC
680 Second Street, San Francisco, California 94107

www.chroniclekids.com

Bagel's LUCKY HAT

book by Hector Mumbly

featuring
Bagel (the dog)
and *Becky* (the cat)

chronicle books · san francisco

Fort Nelson Public Library
Box 330
Fort Nelson, BC
V0C-1R0

Bagel *(the dog)* and Becky *(the cat)*
were winding down for bedtime,

when **suddenly...**

"We were eating pancakes," remembered Bagel. "I wasn't wearing my hat *then*..."

"Well," interrupted Becky, "*that* was easy—you must have misplaced your hat even before we left the *house* this morning!"

"No, no, you didn't let me *finish*," said Bagel.

"When we ***left*** this morning I put my lucky hat on, same as always."

"And I was still wearing it when we got to the park. Becky, **you** played on the *springy-beetle* and I went to the stream at the edge of the park. And then..." continued Bagel...

I sat next to the stream and said **hi** to the fishes.

But then my lucky hat fell right **in**. It floated really far out, really **fast!**

I couldn't reach it, so I jumped off the bank and landed *inside* my lucky hat!

SPLASH

The current carried me downstream. I enjoyed the ride, laughing along with all the laughing fishes, bobbing back and forth.

"Okay: 'LAUGHING FISHES?'" interrupted Becky.

"Really, Becky! Let me *finish*," demanded Bagel.

The stream led to a vast meadow. I paddled to land, put on my **damp** lucky hat, and said good-bye to the fishes.

Then I met a flock of birds. They seemed friendly, so I decided to run after them.

They flew away, then landed. So I chased after them again — and they flew away again.

(It went on like that for a while.)

In the middle of the game, a sudden gust of wind blew my lucky hat **high** above the ground.

WOOSH

I chased after it, but it went **too high.** Just when I was about to give up...

... the flock of birds snatched me up and we retrieved my **LUCKY HAT!** I saw the world from a whole new point of view—**a million miles high!!**

Eventually, the birds set me down by a little shack.

Then a low, *low* **rummmmmble** frightened off the birds.

I followed the rumbling sound *straight* to the shack...
...and down a dingy old staircase...

There was a friendly-looking scientist eating lunch in the corner, but he didn't even *NOTICE* me because of all the loud clanging down there.

A robot arm accidentally knocked off my lucky hat. So I chased it all over the place. Finally, I caught up with it in some kind of cockpit...

...the cockpit of a HUGE ROBOT SUIT!!
Next thing I knew, I'd accidentally pressed a button with the word LAUNCH written on it. A glass dome locked into place around me and the suit's JETPACK ignited!

I took the controls—*soon mastering their intricacies*—weaving wildly between comets and through gas clouds. The distant stars twinkled brightly...

"Baaaa-gellllll!" groaned Becky.

"Wait, wait, it gets **better!**" said Bagel excitedly.

I noticed the fuel gauge was blinking so I set down on a nearby planet.

I don't mean to **brag**, but touchdown was **quite soft** for a beginner.

I hopped out and introduced myself to Norb and Gilletspo.

"I'm out of fuel," I said.

"Too bad we don't use the same kind of fuel here on ZORGONOGON 14," said Norb.

"We can give you a lift back to Earth though," offered Gilletspo.

So we all piled into their comfy, mid-sized flying saucer and **zoooooomed** through space, all the way back to Earth!

"THAT'S IT!" screeched Bagel. "I wasn't wearing my hat on the page before this! **SEE?!** So I must have left it on **ZORGONOGON 14!!**"

"Do you expect me to *believe* all that?" asked Becky. "Let me tell you something: If you ever forget something somewhere, you should *never* think that you have to make up a **STORY** to hide your mistake. Personally, I feel that blah blah blah..."

But before Becky could finish, their mom called out, "Bagel, you have visitors."

"Hey, Bagel. Here's your lucky hat. You forgot it on *ZORGONOGON 14*."

"Oh, thanks, Gilletspo—now I can **sleep**," said Bagel, bouncing into bed.

"Good night, Becky," said Norb and Gilletspo on their way out the door.

the End!